Kylie Jean

Blueberry Queen

by Marci Peschke

illustrated by Tuesday Mourning

PICTURE WINDOW BOOKS

a capstone imprint

Kylie Jean is published by Picture Window Books
A Capstone Imprint
1710 Roe Crest Drive
North Mankato, Minnesota 56003
www.capstonepub.com

Library of Congress Cataloging-in-Publication Data
Peschke, M. (Marci).
  Blueberry queen / by Marci Peschke ; illustrated by Tuesday Mourning.
     p. cm. — (Kylie Jean)
  ISBN 978-1-4048-6756-7 (library binding) — ISBN 978-1-4048-6615-7 (pbk.)
  [1. Beauty contests—Fiction. 2. Texas—Fiction.] I. Mourning, Tuesday, ill. II. Title.
  PZ7.P441245Bl 2011
  [Fic]—dc22   2010030657

Summary: It's time for the annual Blueberry Festival, and Kylie Jean just knows she'd
be the perfect Blueberry Queen.

Creative Director: Heather Kindseth
Graphic Designer: Emily Harris
Editor: Beth Brezenoff
Production Specialist: Michelle Biedscheid

Design Element Credit:
Shutterstock/blue67design

Printed in the United States of America in Stevens Point, Wisconsin.
022014
008035 / 008034

Dedicated to my little queen, Kylie Jean

—MP

Table of Contents

All About Me, Kylie Jean!

My name is Kylie Jean Carter. I live in a big, sunny, yellow house on Peachtree Lane in Jacksonville, Texas with Momma, Daddy, and my two brothers, T.J. and Ugly Brother.

T.J. is my older brother, and Ugly Brother is . . . well . . . he's really a dog. Don't you go telling him he is a dog. Okay? I mean it. He thinks he is a real true person.

He is a black-and-white bulldog. His front looks like his back, all smashed in. His face is all droopy like he's sad, but he's not.

His two front teeth stick out, and his tongue hangs down. (Now you know why his name is Ugly Brother.)

Everyone I love to the moon and back lives in Jacksonville. Nanny, Pa, Granny, Pappy, my aunts, my uncles, and my cousins all live here. I'm extra lucky, because I can see all of them any time I want to!

My momma says I'm pretty. She says I have eyes as blue as the summer sky and a smile as sweet as an angel. (Momma says pretty is as pretty does. That means being nice to the old folks, taking care of little animals, and respecting my momma and daddy.)

But I'm pretty on the outside and on the inside. My hair is long, brown, and curly.

I wear it in a ponytail sometimes, but my absolute most favorite is when Momma pulls it back in a princess style on special days.

I just gave you a little hint about my big dream. Ever since I was a bitty baby I have wanted to be an honest-to-goodness beauty queen. I even know the wave. It's side to side, nice and slow, with a dazzling smile. I practice all the time, because everybody knows beauty queens need to have a perfect wave.

I'm Kylie Jean, and I'm going to be a beauty queen. Just you wait and see!

Chapter One

Going to the Farm

The sun is so hot today! My can of orange soda started getting warm as soon as I walked out of the Drive-N-Go with Momma. We're going to the farm to help Nanny and Pa pick blueberries in the blueberry patch. My cousin Lucy will be there too. She and I like to pick a few and eat a few.

We climb back in the van and the heat sucks all the air outta me like a popped balloon, so I sip my orange soda long and slow.

Momma is busy driving, but I'm busy thinking about being a beauty queen.

My brother T.J. says they don't let little girls be beauty queens, but T.J. is only right half the time. That means I have a chance. Ugly Brother doesn't say much about it. He usually doesn't say much about anything.

Before long, Momma turns on Lickskillet Road, and we can see the farm. Nanny and Pa have a red house and a red barn. They have horses, a huge garden, and a pond. It is magnificent!

Pa is standing in the blueberry patch. He shouts, "Where y'all been? I've been workin' since the rooster crowed."

"Oh Daddy, you know I have things to do at home, too," Momma tells Pa, smiling at him as we climb out of the car. "I've been tryin' out my new recipes for the Blueberry Bake-Off."

She laughs and adds, "Don't you go worrying now, Pa, I won't make you wait two weeks for the Blueberry Festival to try it. I brought you a piece."

My cousin Lucy runs over. "Let's go play!" she says. Then she reaches for my orange soda. "Come on, Kylie Jean!" she shouts. "Just one sip! Pleeease." But I frown and pull it away from her.

Momma turns. She says, "Kylie Jean, you share that soda with your cousin. Pretty is as pretty does." Momma has her arms crossed. That's how I know she means business.

I crinkle up my face a little, but I give Lucy a sip of my orange soda. Then we smile and head over to sit in the shade of a big tree.

Pretty soon, Pa calls us over to the big green tractor. He asks, "Who wants the first ride?"

Lucy and I look at each other. She knows I want
the first ride. "Kylie Jean,
since you gave me a sip of
your orange soda, I want
you to take the first turn,"
Lucy says sweetly. Then we
hug.

I climb up on the tractor
and sit in front of Pa on the
big seat. The tractor starts
up, and it's loud, like T.J.'s lawnmower gone crazy.
Pa begins to drive out to the pond, and I wave just
like a real beauty queen. The tractor is loud, but I
pretend I'm in a parade.

The pond is deep, blue, and perfectly round.
Just like the blueberries in the blueberry patch.

Suddenly an idea strikes my brain just like lightning. I could be the Blueberry Festival Queen!

The rest of the day, I spend my time picking blueberries and dreaming about being a beauty queen.

Chapter Two
Making a Plan

I need a plan if I'm going to be the Blueberry Queen.

One thing I know for sure about making a plan is that you need another person. Pa always says that two heads are better than one.

So on Saturday morning, I wake up real bright and early. Before I go downstairs to eat my blueberry pancakes, I start working on my plan.

First things first, I try to think of a person to help me.

The first person I think of is my cousin Lucy. The problem is, Lucy's just a kid, like me. She won't be able to help me. Plus, she's kind of shy, and I need someone brave.

But Lucy has a big sister, Lilly. Lilly is good at figuring things out, so I give her a call on her cell phone.

She says, "Hey, Kylie Jean, what's up? I'm at cheerleading practice. Is everything okay?"

"I need help with a special beauty queen project," I tell her. "Can you help me?"

Lilly laughs. "Oh, aren't you somethin'? Are you still stuck on being a beauty queen?" she asks.

I'm not so sure that's funny. I wait a second, and then ask, "Are you still stuck on being a cheerleader?"

For a second, she gets kinda quiet. Then she says, "Okay, I see your point. When can I come over?"

"How about now?" I say.

Lilly laughs. "I'm busy right now, sugar," she whispers. I hear a whistle blow. "I'll be at your house at 2," Lilly says. Then she hangs up.

I already have a partner, and I didn't even eat breakfast yet! My plan is going just perfectly.

After I eat my cereal, I spend the morning helping our neighbor, Miss Clarabelle, weed her flowerbeds.

It's a good thing it ain't too hot yet, since weeding can be hard work. I think I could wilt just like one of those flowers.

Miss Clarabelle and I sit on the ground and look real careful. Finding weeds is like finding a bug in a rug. She's wearing a really big purple hat and purple gardening gloves. Purple is her color.

I'm wearing my pink tennis shoes and a pair of gloves with pink bows. You guessed it! Pink is my color.

After pulling so many weeds, I'm covered with dirt. I tell Miss Clarabelle that I have a special meeting today, and I have to quit working. "But I'll come back soon and help you out again," I add.

Miss Clarabelle never stops pulling the weeds. She just says, "You run on, sugar. You've been a lot of help to me today."

I wave to her purple hat and run home across the yard, careful not to step in the flowers. Miss Clarabelle would say a crushed flower is a powerful sad thing.

I take a bath and put on a fancy dress. I want to look my best. When Lilly sees me looking so pretty, she'll know I mean business.

Once I'm ready, I sit quietly in our fancy living room, which is right next to the front door. That's where I'll wait for my cousin.

I sit on the sofa, waiting for Lilly. I hear Momma's tall clock tick . . . tock . . . tick . . . tock. Then I cross my arms just like Momma does when she's waiting for something and it's taking too long.

After a hundred years, the front door opens.

Lilly shouts, "Hey y'all, anyone here? Kylie Jean?" She doesn't see me waiting in the living room.

I don't shout back. Momma says shouting is not ladylike, and right now I'm trying my hardest to be a beauty queen. So instead of yelling, I gracefully hop off the sofa and walk over to the front door.

When I tap her on the back, Lilly lets out a scream! Then she spins around and says, "Kylie Jean, you scared the life outta me!"

When we're done laughing, Lilly looks me over, top to toe. I cross my arms again and smile as she notices my pretty dress.

Lilly nods. "I see that you're serious about this," she says.

"I am," I say. I grab her hand and ask, "What do we do first?"

Chapter Three
Lilly's List

"Let's use T.J.'s computer," Lilly says.

I know that's a bad idea. Before I can stop myself, I snort. I put my hand over my mouth. Beauty queens do not snort!

"What's so funny?" Lilly asks.

"You can use the computer if you can stand the smell in T.J.'s room," I say. "Momma says it stinks worse than the pigsty down at Pa's farm."

Lilly makes a face and pulls her shirt up over her nose. Her eyes are laughing.

She says, "Okay, let's do this."

We push open the door and climb over T.J.'s dirty clothes, sports stuff, and smelly shoes. They cover the floor. I wave at T.J.'s sleeping hamster in its cage.

His computer screen is black. Lilly jiggles the mouse and the screen lights up with a picture of the Dallas Cowboys. Lilly goes on the Internet and types some stuff. Then she prints something out.

"This is the form you need to fill out to sign up for the pageant," Lilly tells me. She sees me looking confused and adds, "The pageant is the beauty queen competition."

"Right," I say. "I know that." Lilly winks.

We go back to the fancy living room.

"First things first," Lilly says, sounding just like Momma when she says it. "We need to make a list."

"What about that form?" I ask.

Lilly waves her hand. "We can fill that out later," she tells me. She points at the paper. "There's some other stuff you're gonna need first."

I lean over to look at the paper.

Lilly glances at me. Then she reads aloud, "All applicants for the Blueberry Queen must have the following: a sponsor, an entry fee of twenty-five dollars, a recent photo, posters, a recommendation letter, a three-hundred-word essay, and their own transportation."

My mouth drops open.

"Are you serious?" I whisper.

Twenty-five dollars? Where am I supposed to get that? And I don't even know what the rest of that stuff is. Being a beauty queen sounds way harder than I thought!

Lilly sits back on the sofa and stares at me. "Well, that's quite a list, Kylie Jean," she says. She puts her hand under her chin. I'm waiting for her to say something. All of a sudden, she looks at her watch. "Oh, I gotta run. I'll help you out another time, okay?"

"What about the form?" I ask her. I'm feeling nervous. This is an awful lot of stuff to do!

"Don't worry," she says. "I'll help you fill it out."

Just then, her cell phone rings. The ring sounds like a song from the KICK country radio station.

Lilly flips her phone open and says, "Hey. I'm on my way." She nods her head a lot and says, "Hmm, yeah, okay." Then she closes her phone and stuffs it in her pocket.

"I gotta scoot," Lilly says. She grabs her cheerleading bag on the way to the front door. Then she gives me a wink and says, "Let me know when you get a sponsor."

"Okay," I tell her. There is one teensy tiny problem. I have no idea what a sponsor is.

I look out the window and watch as Lilly runs down the driveway to her car.

I'm still sitting on the sofa thinking about the sponsor when T.J. comes in. He says, "Hey lil' bit, what you doin' lookin' all fancy?"

I ignore the question since I have one of my own. "T.J., what is a sponsor?" I ask.

He answers, "Someone who helps you out, you know, gives you money and stuff. Racecar drivers all get sponsors. Why?" He's looking at me funny.

I smile sweetly and say, "No reason. Just askin' so I'll know."

Now his face is all twisted up. He asks, "So you'll know what?"

"Silly!" I say. "So I'll know what a sponsor does." T.J. knows a lot, but sometimes he just doesn't pay much attention.

Chapter Four
Pa to the Rescue

I need a sponsor, and I got an idea about how
to get one. To do it, I have to wait till we go to
Nanny and Pa's house for Sunday dinner. I hate
waiting. I keep telling myself, "First things first."
But I'm in an awful big hurry to be a beauty
queen!

Finally, Sunday comes. As soon as I get to
Nanny and Pa's big red house after church, I see
Lucy. I can't wait to change and play with her. I
run inside to put on my overalls. Momma doesn't
want me to get my nice clothes dirty.

When I come back outside, more cousins and aunts and uncles are there. The older girls are helping Nanny, Momma, and the aunts with the food. Pa, Daddy, and the uncles have set old doors up like tables and put folding chairs out. Lilly is fixing glasses of sweet tea.

My cousin Jake rings the old black iron dinner bell in the backyard. The kids all come running to the table. It's loaded with fried chicken, rolls, purple hull peas, mashed taters, sliced tomaters, watermelon, and homemade fruit pies. Yum!

We fix our plates, and then Pa says a blessing. Then we can dig in!

We're all laughing and eating and talking. Jake tells funny jokes. The grown-ups are all talking about boring stuff like work.

I don't pay attention until I hear the aunts talking about the Blueberry Festival. They're all wondering who will be the next queen.

"I heard Maggie Lou Butler is goin' for it," I hear Momma say. "And she is right pretty, and a nice girl too." Now I'm listening to every word, but quick as a jackrabbit, they start talking about prices at the Piggly Wiggly. Lilly turns her head toward me and smiles secretly.

After we eat, Nanny and Pa walk over to their swing. They like to sit there together just like the true sweethearts they are.

I make my way over, hoping no one else follows me.

"Hello, Kylie Jean," Pa says.

Without waiting, I say, "Pa, I got a business deal for you." I'm pretty nervous and excited about my plan. I hop up and down on one leg.

Pa smiles. "Do you now, Miss Kylie Jean?" he asks. "I guess you better tell me about it quick, before you burst your bubble from sheer excitement."

"Well," I begin, "don't you want Lickskillet Farm to be famous?"

"We're famous enough already," Nanny says.

"If you were to sponsor me in the Blueberry Festival pageant," I tell her, "I could put Lickskillet Farm on ALL of my posters. Your farm would be extra famous!"

Nanny frowns. She asks, "Did you ask your momma about this, sugar?"

I shake my head and say, "No ma'am. It is a for sure surprise."

When Pa laughs, it rumbles from deep in his belly. His eyes laugh, too. He pulls a wad of money out of his pocket. Then he tells me, "Kylie Jean, you sure are somethin' else. How much money are we talkin' about here?"

"Twenty-five dollars," I tell him. "But I'm not somethin' else. I'm goin' to be the next Blueberry Queen!"

Pa smiles and hands me the money. "Thank you, Pa," I say sweetly. I kiss his cheek. As I walk away, I stuff the money in my pocket. Then I take out my list. I can cross off "Sponsor" and "25 Dollars." I'm on my way!

Chapter Five
Fairy Garden Picture

The next thing on my list is "photo," so when I get up the next day, I start looking for my photo. I look in Momma's room for the box of pictures.

When I find the box, I dump the pictures out on the floor, so I can look at them carefully. Suddenly I hear a sound.

It sounds like a pig.

Ugly Brother is standing at the door. His pink tongue is dripping with doggie drool, and doggie drool and photos do NOT go together. I jump up and grab him by the collar.

Staring into his eyes, I tell him, "Ugly Brother, I know you came to help me be a beauty queen, but this is not the way you can help me out. You have to wait until I tell you a job to do."

Ugly Brother says, "Ruff, ruff." He knows the plan. I let go and he sits down to watch me.

I look at all of the pictures. Momma has millions of baby pictures of me, T.J., and Ugly Brother. Some of them are pretty cute. In some of them, my face is all red and squished.

I show Ugly Brother pictures of him as a bitty baby. He tries to lick one.

I quickly pull the picture away and say, "No licking! Just looking!" Then he puts his head under his paw.

There are pictures of Daddy and T.J. fishing. There are pictures of me, T.J., and Ugly Brother on Halloween, when I was dressed as a fairy princess. That would've been perfect, except that was the year T.J. went dressed as some kind of turtle. None of these pictures are right.

Suddenly an idea hits me like a brick. I need Pappy!

Pappy loves to take pictures. He even used to do it for a job. He has a black room to make pictures in and everything.

I know I'll need an extra-special outfit for my picture. I put on a pink dress with a huge pink fluffy skirt, my fairy wings from Halloween, a flower crown with long ribbons, and my white shiny shoes with tiny heels.

I look in Momma's little hand mirror.

There is strawberry jelly on my face. "Oops!" I say. I spit on my finger and wipe it off.

Then I look myself up and down and say, "Perfect!"

Ugly Brother is sitting in the doorway. He says, "Ruff, ruff."

Two barks is yes and one bark is no. That means I'm ready to go. "Momma," I yell, "I'm goin' to Pappy's house."

"All right," she calls back. "Don't get in the way, and come home for lunch."

"Yes ma'am," I holler.

Careful not to slam the door behind me, I run outside. I jump on my hot pink bike and pedal down the street.

Granny and Pappy live way down at the other end of Peachtree Lane. Their house is tall, old, and the color of the sky on a sunny day. That's where my daddy grew up.

I ring the bell at the front door. When Pappy opens the door, he smiles at me and says, "It's nice to see you, love bug. But Granny is at the garden club meeting. They're having a speaker on herbs today."

"I came to see you, Pappy," I tell him. "Can you take a special picture of me in Granny's rose garden?"

He smiles real big and
pats me on my head.
"Reckon I can," he says.
"Meet me 'round back in
the garden."

Pappy takes my picture on the swing, under the arbor, and on the bench in front of the pink rose bushes. The pink roses are the same color as my pink dress.

I smile for every picture, and Pappy tells me, "You're the prettiest girl I ever did see."

"Thanks, Pappy," I tell him.

When we're done, Pappy says, "All right, little miss. Come back tomorrow, and we'll see how they look."

"Don't tell a soul," I whisper. "This is top-secret beauty queen work."

He nods, waves, and goes inside the big blue house with his camera.

Chapter Six
Poster Party

When I get home from Pappy's, I ask Momma if my friends can come over. "I want to have a paintin' party after lunch," I explain.

I don't tell her that I want to make posters for the Blueberry Queen Festival. Posters are the next thing on my list.

"That's real nice, but don't you make a big mess now, Kylie Jean," Momma tells me.

"No ma'am," I say. "I sure don't want to make a big mess." Then I run into the kitchen to call all of my friends.

While I eat my chicken salad sandwich and drink my cold milk, I make a plan.

As soon as my friends get here, we will make a line. Each girl will have a job. I need to make the first poster so that we can make lots of copies of it. I have to have lots of posters, so the judges will see them and choose me as Blueberry Queen.

As soon as Momma goes out to work in the yard, I make my poster. It's pink, of course! That's my color.

In the middle of the poster is a giant blue circle with a smiley face. The blueberry is wearing a gold glitter crown. Underneath the blueberry, I write, "Vote Kylie Jean for Blueberry Queen!" Except I spell blueberry wrong and have to X it out and write it again.

At the bottom of the poster, I draw a big green tractor. Next to the tractor, in smaller letters, I write, "Sponsored by Lickskillet Farm." I had to ask Miss Clarabelle earlier how to spell sponsored.

Soon, the doorbell rings. Then I hear giggles and loud talking. I run downstairs to greet my friends.

Lucy comes in first. Then Kristy, Cara, Katie, and Daisy follow her.

Once they're all in my house, I say, "Ladies, we've got work to do." I take them up to my room and carefully shut the door behind them.

"You're about to see something amazing," I say. Then I show them the poster.

They love it!

Daisy says, "Kylie Jean, you know blue is my color. Please, please let me make the big blue circles."

"Okay," I say. "Who writes nice and pretty?" Kristy raises her hand real slow.

"This is goin' better than I planned it," I say. "Kristy, you do the writin' on the top and bottom of the poster."

Katie decides she'll make the smiley faces on the blue circles. "Why'd you make your face blue?" she asks me. "Are you supposed to be from outer space or somethin' like that?"

Cara laughs. "Silly! That there is a blueberry. Right, Kylie Jean?"

"You got it!" I say. "You're smart."

Cara says, "I'll use the glitter pen to make the sparkly crown, because I'm so smart. I'm a superstar!"

We all laugh. "I'll do the tractors," I tell them. "Let's get started."

Daisy starts making a big blue circle on one poster. Then she passes it to Kristy, who will add the writing.

I'm at the end, so I have to wait for the first poster to go all the way through the line before it gets to me.

Then I notice something. Kristy spelled the word blueberry wrong (like blubery) and put a big X over it, just like I did.

"Stop!" I yell.

"What's wrong?" Kristy asks. "I'm making it just like you did!"

I sigh. "I know," I say. "But you don't have to write it the wrong way. Spell blueberry right on all the posters. Okay?"

She nods her head yes and starts to write again.

After about an hour we have a whole pile of pink posters. Cara asks, "So, where are you gonna put all your pretty posters? If it was me, I would put one at the Piggly Wiggly grocery store."

Daisy says, "How about the Drive-N-Go?"

Katie says, "How 'bout taking them to church?"

Kristy says, "I think you should put one at the courthouse."

Lucy says, "Take some posters downtown."

We're a great team. I love my friends!

Then Momma calls, "Y'all come down. I've got hot chocolate chip cookies and ice cold lemonade."

Daisy shouts, "Yum-o!" We all run for the door.

I'm glad my posters are done. But there's so much  left on my list. I don't have much time till the Blueberry Festival. I've been saving one of the hardest things for last.

I have to write an essay!

Chapter Seven
The Letter

When I wake up the next day, I get going even before I have breakfast. The first thing I have to do today is see the pictures that Pappy took. I need to pick one to send in with my application for Blueberry Queen.

I stroll over to Pappy's house. When I get there, I ring the doorbell that sounds like a church bell.

Granny comes to the door. She asks, "Are you here to see Pappy and get your pictures?"

"Yup!" I answer.

Pappy calls for me to come to the kitchen. My pictures are all on the table.

When I see them, I can't help it: I shout with joy. Then I whisper, "Pappy, you made me look sweet as an angel!"

After looking at each picture, I choose the one with the best smile.

Pappy agrees. "That's my favorite one too, little miss," he says. Then he adds, "You know I like to take your picture, so you ask me anytime."

I give my pappy some sugar and say thank you before I go.

I'm in a hurry to get home. Another project is waiting for me.

I need help on my essay. And to help me, I need someone who knows a lot of words. Maybe even a million words. Lucky for me, I know just the right person to help me.

As soon as I get home, I run upstairs to my room and find my pink notebook and my pink pen with the long feather on it.

"Momma!" I holler. "I'm goin' to Miss Clarabelle's house."

"Don't bug her," Momma says.

"I won't!" I call as I slam the front door.

I carefully run across the yard, because I do not want to step on any of the beautiful flowers. They look like a quilt tucking Miss Clarabelle's house into the green grass.

When Miss Clarabelle opens the door, she smiles.

"I need help, ma'am," I say.

She waves her hand and I follow her to the fancy living room. Miss Clarabelle calls it the parlor. Like I said, she knows a lot of words!

Miss Clarabelle sits down in a big, soft, purple chair. Then she pats the footstool in front of her. "Come and sit," she says. After I make myself comfortable, she asks me, "How can I help you, Kylie Jean?"

I explain all of my writing troubles to her and I can tell she's listening because she looks at my face when I'm talking and she nods her head at all the right times.

Then I say, "The worst part is, I need a commendation. I don't even know what one is."

She laughs. It sounds like a little tinkling bell. "Do you mean a recommendation?" she asks.

Miss Clarabelle explains that a recommendation is just a letter of kind words in support of someone. She tells me lots of folks need them to get a job. I wonder if Daddy needed one to get his job at the newspaper.

I think real hard, and my forehead gets wrinkly. I squeeze my eyes tight. Then an idea jumps right on me like a flea.

I take a deep breath. Then I say, "Miss Clarabelle, would you do me the honor of writing my recommendation to be Blueberry Queen?"

She smiles and says, "I would be delighted to write a letter supporting you as the next queen."

"I got another problem I need your help with, ma'am," I say quietly. "I have to write an essay. And it has to have three hundred words in it!"

"My goodness," Miss Clarabelle says. "That is a long essay for someone your age. But I think you can do it."

"How do I get started?" I ask.

"Well, the first thing you should do is make a list of all of the reasons you want to be Blueberry Queen," Miss Clarabelle tells me.

"My reasons are I want to be a queen, I'm right pretty, and I like blueberries," I tell her.

Miss Clarabelle laughs. "I think you may need a few more things than that," she says. "Why don't you think of about five more reasons you'll be a great Blueberry Queen. Then you can start on your essay. I'll get to work on your letter."

She starts working on my recommendation. I can hear her fancy pen scratching across the paper. While she writes, I work on my list.

When I get bored of that, I draw blueberries on the paper.

After about a hundred minutes she puts down the pen. Then she hands me the letter.

To whom it may concern:

I am writing this letter to recommend Miss Kylie Jean Carter for Blueberry Queen. I have known this young lady from the day she was born. It is her life-long goal and dream to be a queen. I have watched her work in my garden and flowerbeds, so I know she likes growing things. I also know that she works hard and is willing to get dirty if the job calls for it. She is nice and kind. Kylie Jean has many supporters, and we would love to see her at the front of the Blueberry Festival parade.

I cannot think of a better young lady to be our next Blueberry Queen. Thank you!

Yours Sincerely,

Miss Clarabelle Lee

I can feel tears prickling in my eyes as I jump up and throw my arms around her neck. I squeeze her in a big hug.

"Miss Clarabelle," I say, "you went and made me cry with your words. Your letter will make those judges choose me. I just know it for sure!"

Chapter Eight
Three Hundred Words

Back at home, I sneak up to T.J.'s room. Ugly Brother follows me and sits down beside the desk. I push all the junk off of T.J.'s desk chair and sit down. The computer is already on, so I get right to work.

First things first, I think about my list. I write all my ideas on a blank piece of paper from the printer.

I begin. I delete. I begin again. I keep writing until my essay is done. Then I read it out loud to Ugly Brother.

Why I Want to be Blueberry Queen

By Kylie Jean Carter

Ever since I was a bitty baby I knew I wanted to be a beauty queen. It is my big dream in life. Being a queen is important work. I know because I've watched Miss America every year since I was two. I know the beauty queen wave too. Nice and slow, a side to side wave. You will not find a young lady for your queen who has more sparkle than me.

I have all the right stuff to be your new Blueberry Queen. My nanny and pa are my sponsors. They own world-famous Lickskillet Farm. My pink Kylie Jean for Blueberry Queen posters are all over town. I have included a picture my pappy took of me in the rose garden.

As you can see I am wearing my flower crown, but I am sure the picture would be even better if I had a real crown to wear, so just pretend I have one on. Okay?

A lot of pretty girls will enter your beauty queen contest, but I am so very pretty. My eyes are as blue as the summer sky and my hair is long, brown, and curly. Everyone knows a beautiful smile can make a queen. Don't you worry! I always brush my teeth every day, so they are white as my momma's pearl necklace.

Speaking of my momma, she likes to say, "Kylie Jean, pretty is as pretty does." This makes me think that I have to be nice on my insides to be pretty on my outsides. I am smart and I work real hard. Plus, I try to be nice all the time.

Finally, the last thing I want to say is that I just love blueberries! I know these things will make you decide that I am the very best choice for your new queen.

When I get done reading, Ugly Brother says, "Ruff, ruff." That means he thinks it is really good. I'm glad.

Chapter Nine
A Ride

After I finish my essay, I look at the next thing on my list. I need to get some transportation. I'm thinking about using my pink bike, but it will be hard to hold the handlebars and wave real pretty to the crowd.

I can tell Ugly Brother thinks it is a bad idea too, so I ask him. I say, "Ugly Brother, do you think I should ride my bike in the parade?"

He says, "Ruff." That means no.

All of a sudden an idea hits my brain like dew on grass.

"Ugly Brother," I say, "I'm surely goin' to need your help."

He says, "Ruff, ruff." That means yes!

Ugly Brother follows me to the garage. I pull out my old red wagon and a small stool. I put the stool inside the wagon. Then I climb inside the wagon and wave nice and slow, side to side.

This just might work!

Ugly Brother puts his face under his paw and whines. He seems nervous.

"Don't worry, Ugly Brother," I say. "I'm not done yet."

Next I go inside. I get one of Momma's old blue sheets, a pair of scissors, and a blue pillow off of T.J.'s bed. I cut the sheet so I can put it over the stool and wagon. Then I cut a big round hole in the center of the dark blue pillow.

I look at Ugly Brother and say, "When I get through with you, you're gonna look just like a big ole blueberry."

Ugly Brother puts his other paw over his face and whines louder. I sit down on the ground beside him.

"You're not gonna like this," I tell him, "but face it, you're not so handsome, Ugly Brother. This is gonna make you look real nice."

It takes me a long time, but I finally get the pillow pulled up around his middle. Ugly Brother stands real still. The blue pillow is like a giant blue inner tube around his middle.

He has white pillow stuffing stuck to his pink tongue, and one of his ears is bent back from me pushing him into the pillow.

I shake my head and put my hands on my hips. "It's your own fault you got stuffin' on your tongue," I tell him. "You should have put it in your mouth."

He tries to sit down, but the pillow gets in the way.

"No sitting down on the job, Ugly Brother," I scold him. "You have to pull this wagon." I tie him up to the handle of the wagon.

Then I shout, "Go to Granny and Pappy's house, Ugly Brother!" He starts to pull me, real slow like. I smile and wave.

I think I have sunburn by the time we get to the end of the street. We've been moving slow as molasses. Ugly Brother has had several resting times along the way. I don't think he will make it down all the streets on the day of the parade.

Granny and Pappy are sitting on their porch. I wave when I get closer.

Pappy says, "Kylie Jean, just what are you doin' to that poor dog? And what is he wearin'?"

"I need transportation," I explain. "And my transportation is wearin' a blueberry costume."

Granny runs inside the house and then comes back with a bowl of cold water for Ugly Brother. She says, "He must be burnin' up dressed up like that, poor boy."

She starts to laugh again and has tears in her eyes. "Pappy, come help us get this pillow off of this dog!" she says.

After he gets Ugly Brother out of the pillow, Pappy looks me in the eye. "Listen, love bug," he says. "If they pick you for Blueberry Queen, I have a fancy old car that will make it down the street better than Ugly Brother here."

I can't believe it! "Yippee!" I shout.

Then I look to make sure no one else but Granny and Pappy heard me shouting. I hug Pappy real hard.

He asks, "Is that the best bear hug you've got?"

"Yup!" I tell him, but I squeeze him even tighter.

Chapter Ten
Finally Done

On Wednesday morning, I wake up early. The house is full up with the smell of blueberry muffins. Momma must be trying another new recipe for the Blueberry Bake-Off. She only has a few days left before the festival.

Every year since I can remember, my momma has won a blue first-place ribbon for her cooking. She has the ribbons pinned all over the inside of our pantry door.

I stretch. I yawn. The sun is up, and today is going to be a great day.

My plan is to finish my beauty queen list.

Suddenly an idea hits my brain like chocolate syrup on ice cream. Maybe my list is all done!

- [x] Sponsor
- [x] twenty-five dollars
- [x] a recent photo
- [x] posters
- [x] a recommendation letter
- [x] a 300-word essay
- [x] transportation
- [ ] application

I can check off everything on my list but the application. I shout, "Yippee!"

Ugly Brother agrees. He says, "Ruff, ruff."

Before I even get dressed, I go downstairs to get the phone and call Lilly. At first, I can't find the phone. After I look all over the den, I find it in the couch cushions. This means T.J. was talking on the phone. He never puts it back on the charger. I dial Lilly's cell phone.

Lilly answers. "Hey girl, what's up?" She's getting ready to go to cheer camp, so I make it quick.

"Lilly, my list is done!" I tell her. "I have everything you told me to get. Do you have my application ready?"

I hear Lilly slamming her car door. She asks, "Do you have a sponsor?"

"Sure do," I say. "Nanny and Pa."

Lilly laughs and says, "Good job, little cousin. Are you sure you have everything on the list?"

"Yes!" I tell her.

Lilly tells me that she will come by in the afternoon to pick up all of my papers and send my application. I'm really on my way to being the Blueberry Queen!

Chapter Eleven
An Extra-Elegant Dress

After dinner, it's time to tell Momma my big news. I go to the kitchen. Momma is doing dishes in her apron with the blueberries on it.

"Momma, I have a surprise," I say. "I've been workin' on something you don't know about. Nanny, Pa, T.J., Ugly Brother, Lilly, Lucy, Granny, Pappy, and my friends all helped me send in my papers to be the Blueberry Queen."

Momma's eyes get big, and she sits down in a chair at the kitchen table. She says, "Well I do declare, Kylie Jean, that is a big surprise!"

I sit beside Momma and tell her all about the pageant. She looks at me and smiles. Then she says, "Honey, you are going to need a dress. We will need your granny to help us pick one out. I better call her and see if she can go with us tomorrow."

The next day we go to Jefferson to buy my dress at the Elegance Dress Shop. It takes a long time to drive to Jefferson, but I'm gonna need an extra-special elegant dress. On the way, Momma tells Granny all about the tasty blueberry treats she has been making and how she is after another blue ribbon this year.

When we turn onto Old Jacksonville Road, I know we are getting close. Every bit of me is on edge with excitement.

Then Momma says to Granny, "Let's go to Ms. Pauline's Tearoom and eat lunch first."

I can't believe it! How can they be thinking about eating lunch now? We are almost there.

Momma's van pulls right into the tearoom parking lot. Ms. Pauline has her tearoom in a big old house. Granny says, "I just love the chicken salad here." The last thing I can think about is eating. I want to pick out my dress!

We go inside the old house and sit at a table. The waitress comes and takes our order. We all have chicken salad sandwiches with fresh fruit. I have milk, but the grown-ups have sweet tea.

I eat fast, but Momma and Granny take their time. While I wait, I look around and see lots of ladies with big tea hats.

Usually going to Ms. Pauline's is a special treat, but today I would have rather had a Happy Meal if it meant we'd get my dress right away.

Our next stop is the Elegance Dress Shop. Out front there's a big fancy sign with letters that have lots of curls on them. The shop sells a lot of fancy dresses for weddings and parties.

We go inside, and I go to the dressing room. It is big, with a red velvety chair in the corner. I stand there in my slip. Beauty queens always wear a slip because it is classy.

Momma and Granny help me try on about one hundred dresses. I feel like a Barbie doll, the way they keep putting new dresses on me. We try white ones with ruffles, yellow ones the color of soft creamy butter, and a blue one with bows.

There is a big mirror with three pieces of glass. When I stand in the middle, I can see all around me. I twirl in the blue dress.

Granny frowns. She says, "I just don't think we have the right dress yet. You look right pretty, but somehow it just doesn't seem like a winning dress."

Momma agrees. "We best take one more look at the rack."

I keep twirling in front of the mirror.

Finally, Granny brings one more dress for me to try on. It is a light pink color, and it has little white dots all over it. It has white lace, a big white satin bow, and fluffy white net slip to wear under it.

When I come out wearing it, Momma
and Granny are speechless because I look so
beautiful in my dress.

"I feel like a real true beauty queen wearin'
this dress," I tell them.

Momma says, "I think we found the one."

Granny says, "Yes, we surely did!"

I smile and twirl around and around.
Momma buys me the dress and some tights
with little white dots and gloves with white
lace. Now I'm ready for my big day at the
pageant!

Chapter Twelve
The Blueberry Festival

The next day, I'm helping Momma get ready to take her special blueberry pecan granola pie to the festival. My pageant won't be until tomorrow. We load up three big baskets with pies. T.J. carries them to the van.

Momma calls, "Y'all, get in the van."

Ugly Brother has trouble jumping up. He barks and jumps. He gets his front end up, but not his back end. He can't do it, so he covers his face with his paws. I think he's embarrassed.

Daddy picks up Ugly Brother and puts him in the back. We drive as close as we can to the town square. Some of the streets downtown are closed. We are still two blocks from the festival. "We're gonna have to walk," Daddy says.

We all get out of the van and start to walk. We walk past shops, coffee houses, jewelry stores, and the bank. I'm the only one not carrying a pie basket, but I have Ugly Brother's leash.

As we get closer T.J. shouts, "The Blueberry Brothers Bluegrass Band sounds awesome! I just love that banjo playing. Hey, could I sell my guitar and get a banjo?"

Momma says, "T.J., you cannot sell Pa's guitar, but if you have enough saved up then go right on and buy yourself a banjo."

Momma is walking fast. She's worried about being late for the bake-off. Daddy is in a hurry too. He wants to head over to the blueberry pancake breakfast.

We turn the corner and see little white tents all over the place. There are tents selling blueberry jellies, jams, and barbecue sauce. There are tents selling blueberries by the bucket and blueberry plants in big pots. There are tents for contests and events, too. I even see a face-painting tent run by the cheerleaders. Lilly is there. She sees me and waves.

Momma points to one tent and says, "There's the bake-off tent."

Daddy says, "We can drop off these pies and go eat breakfast."

T.J. nods. He says, "I'll eat pancakes right now, but later I'm going to enter the Blue Face Pie-Eating Contest for sure!"

By now, Ugly Brother is pulling me. He is so excited to see all the folks that he keeps trying to run over and say hi to them all. I see Nanny and Pa sitting at a picnic table. They're with Granny and Pappy. Lucy is with them!

My relatives all wave, and I try to wave back, but I need both my hands on the leash now because Ugly Brother is pulling so hard.

We leave the pies at the bake-off tent and go to get our pancakes.

Then we sit with my grandparents and Lucy and eat. Daddy and T.J. eat three plates of blueberry pancakes each.

Some of the blueberries are small as a dime. Some of the pancakes are big as the plate.

The grown-ups are all talking. I can tell Momma is as nervous as a cat in a pool. Cats don't like water one little bit. I don't think I should say how I know.

Lucy asks, "Did you see your pink posters hanging by the courthouse?"

"Yup," I answer. "They look awesome!" I'm finished with my pancakes. "Momma and Daddy, can Lucy and I go run around and have fun?" I ask.

"All by yourselves?" Momma says. "I don't know."

Pa wipes syrup off his face. "I'll go with 'em," he says.

"Yay!" I say. "Let's go!" I grab one of Pa's hands. Lucy grabs the other.

We spend our time visiting all the little tents and getting our faces painted. I get blueberries on my face. Lucy gets them too!

"You girls look right pretty," the face-painting lady tells us.

"Why thank you!" I say.

I love the Blueberry Festival. It is so much fun! I wish it could happen every day during the summer.

Finally, it's time to see who the winner of the bake-off is. We go back to the tables.

Daddy is holding Momma's hand. Momma looks nervous, so I give her a wink. She winks back at me.

Before long, a man in a white suit and cowboy hat steps up to face the crowd. Pa whispers to me, "That man there is the head judge."

The man shouts, "We have the results! Shelly is the winner for her delicious blueberry pecan granola pie."

Shelly is my momma's name! We all cheer and clap for my momma.

Nanny says, "I declare, this is the tenth year in a row you've been number one. You are some cook!"

"She sure is," Daddy says.

Momma jumps up to get her picture taken with the blue ribbon. Today it will sit by her pie so everybody can see it.

I tell Lucy, "Tomorrow, Momma will put her ribbon on the pantry door. You know what else will happen tomorrow?"

Lucy shakes her head. "What?" she asks.

I raise my head proudly and tell her, "Tomorrow, I will be the new Blueberry Queen."

Chapter Thirteen
Time to Shine!

The day of the pageant is finally here. At five o'clock in the morning, I wake up because I can't sleep any more. Then I'm so excited that I can't eat my breakfast.

My stomach feels like T.J.'s pet hamster is running around in it.

When I go downstairs, Momma says, "Kylie Jean, sugar, eat some toast. You don't want to feel sick at the pageant."

"Too late, Momma!" I say. "I already feel sick!"

Momma laughs. She says, "Eat your toast. Just remember, soon-to-be beauty queens do not get nervous."

After I eat my toast, I take a long bubble bath and scrub under my nails and behind my ears. Then I get dressed. First I put on my white tights, then my fluffy white slip, and finally my pretty new pink dress.

Granny and Nanny have come to help me. Nanny buckles my little shiny pink shoes with the tiny heels. Granny pulls my hair back in a princess style.

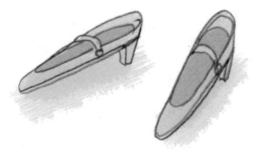

I look in my mirror and see a soon-to-be Blueberry Queen.

Downstairs, everyone is waiting to see me. When I walk in the kitchen, Daddy, Pappy, Pa, T.J., and Ugly Brother all gather around me. I twirl around so they can see my beautiful dress.

Ugly Brother says, "Ruff, ruff."

Daddy says, "Well, sweetheart, don't you look all grown up!"

"She sure does," Pappy says. He looks at the kitchen clock and adds, "We better hit the road or our little miss will be late."

My family gets in the van. The grandparents all ride in Pappy's old car. I feel dizzy the whole way downtown to the Hotel Magnolia.

When we pull in the parking lot, there are about a million cars parked all around the hotel. Daddy helps me get out of the van, and Momma holds my hand.

Normally I would skip all the way inside, but not today. I'm trying to act like a true queen, so I stand straight and tall.

Pa holds the door open and we go inside. The ballroom is right next to us. You should see all the people in there! It is packed full.

Momma takes me to wait in the room next to the ballroom with all the other girls who want to be the Blueberry Queen.

Then I notice something. Everyone else waiting is a grown-up girl! I can't believe it! They are all so fancy.

Maggie Lou Butler is standing right beside me. Her blond hair is fixed up on top of her head. She looks just like a movie star. All these older girls look like movie stars.

I start to get the hiccups. I always get them when I'm scared.

"You just wait a minute, Kylie Jean, you'll be fine," Momma says. "Take a big breath. Remember, this is your dream come true."

Momma is right. In a minute they will call our names, and we will go out and introduce ourselves.

Momma smiles and whispers to me, "Smile, talk slow, and be clear, so they can understand you."

Then I hear a voice. "Kylie Jean Carter." That's me!

I walk into the ballroom and up on the stage. But the microphone is as tall as my momma, and I can't reach.

Everyone laughs. I don't know what to do. I could yell, but that's not how beauty queens act. It wouldn't be right. Luckily, a man runs out and fixes the microphone so I can talk.

"Hello, y'all," I begin. "My name is Kylie Jean Carter, and my sponsor is Lickskillet Farm. Ever since I was a bitty baby, I've been wantin' to be a queen. Please vote for me for your next Blueberry Queen."

Then I wave nice and slow, side to side, the beauty queen wave. I smile real big, too.

Everybody laughs again. Not like they're making fun of me, but like I make them happy.

Then I go and stand in the back of the stage next to Momma. About ten grown-up girls walk out and tell their names. Then we all have to wait to see who the new queen is going to be.

I just know it is going to be me!

Pretty soon, a man comes out on the stage. "Who's that?" I ask Momma.

"That's the head judge," Momma whispers back. "He's going to tell us who the winner is!"

I hold my breath as the man says, "I have the results. It was a very close contest this year."

I feel sorry for those grown-up girls. They're going to be awful sad when I win.

Then the judge announces, "Maggie Lou Butler from Prickly Pear Creek is our new Blueberry Queen!"

Maggie Lou goes to the stage. Everyone is clapping. Momma pats my back.

I think I might cry.

Then the clapping stops. The judge man has something else to say. He looks over at me and says, "For the very first time ever, we have a Little Miss Blueberry Queen. Kylie Jean Carter, come on up here!"

Everyone goes wild! They're all cheering and calling my name. Momma starts crying, so I pat her back. Then I skip all the way to the microphone. The man puts a diamond tiara on my head.

I wave to everyone again. Nice and slow, side to side. For the first time, I'm not just pretending I'm a real, true queen.

I am one.

Chapter Fourteen
The Parade

The day after the pageant, I'm going to be in a parade. I eat a huge breakfast with my family.

Momma says, "Kylie Jean, finish your eggs so you can get dressed."

After T.J. finishes his breakfast, he goes to help Pappy shine up the fancy old car.

Daddy winks at me. "I have a special job to do today," he says.

I look at Momma, but she just shrugs. Daddy is up to something. I just know it.

Momma smiles and says, "When you wear that tiara, you will feel real special."

I get dressed in my special pink dress again. Momma fixes my hair back and puts my tiara on. Then I'm ready to go for a ride in the parade.

Daddy is waiting downstairs. He hands me a big box with a giant bow on the top.

"What is it, Daddy?" I ask.

"Open it and see," he tells me with a wink.

I open up the box. Inside, I find a big ole bunch of pink roses.

Daddy smiles and says, "A queen needs roses, Kylie Jean."

"Oh, Daddy!" I say. "I'm gonna smile and wave and make y'all proud of me."

"We couldn't be any prouder of you than we already are, Kylie Jean," Momma tells me.

I hold the flowers in front of me and wave. Then I ask Ugly Brother, "Do I look like a queen?"

He says, "Ruff, ruff." That means yes!

Out front, Pappy honks the horn of his fancy old car. We all go outside. Pa puts a white fake fur blanket on the back of Pappy's car and lifts me up to sit on it.

I fluff out my skirt and fix my roses. Pa says, "You sure are somethin', Kylie Jean."

I tell him, "I'm not somethin', I'm a Little Miss Blueberry Queen."

Pa smiles. He leans over and taps me on the nose. Then he asks, "Ready, sugar pie?"

"Yes, sir, I surely am," I answer. "Ever since I was a bitty baby."

Pa, Pappy, Daddy, and T.J. get in the car. Pappy drives down our street and turns onto Main Street. I see Miss Clarabelle waving her fan at me. All of my friends are calling my name. Nanny, Granny, and Momma are all blowing kisses to me as I pass by. Ugly Brother is sitting by Momma with his new blue collar, saying, "Ruff, ruff!" to me.

I think I may need a fan club after today.

Being the Little Miss Blueberry Queen made me happier and prouder than anything. Someday I'm going to be a real true beauty queen. I have big plans!

Marci Bales Peschke was born in Indiana, grew up in Florida, and now lives in Texas with her husband, two children, and a feisty black-and-white cat named Phoebe. She loves reading and watching movies.

When **Tuesday Mourning** was a little girl, she knew she wanted to be an artist when she grew up. Now, she is an illustrator who lives in South Pasadena, CA. She especially loves illustrating books for kids and teenagers. When she isn't illustrating, Tuesday loves spending time with her husband, who is an actor, and their two sons.

Glossary

application (ap-luh-KAY-shuhn)—a formal request for something

elegant (EL-uh-guhnt)—graceful and stylish

essay (ESS-ay)—a piece of writing about a particular subject

goal (GOHL)—something that you aim for; a dream

magnificent (mag-NIF-i-sent)—very impressive or beautiful

pageant (PAJ-uhnt)—a contest and performance

project (PROJ-ekt)—something worked on over a period of time

recommendation (rek-uh-mend-AY-shuhn)—a letter written in support of someone else

sponsor (SPON-sur)—someone who gives money and support to another person

transportation (transs-pur-TAY-shuhn)—a way to get from place to place

wilt (WILT)—to begin to droop or become tired

Talk!

1. Lots of people help Kylie Jean achieve her goal. What can you do to help your friends when they have goals? Talk about it.

2. Kylie Jean had a long list of things to do to get ready for the pageant. Which thing was the hardest? Explain your answer.

3. What do you think happens after this story ends?

Available from Picture Window Books
www.capstonepub.com

THE FUN DOESN'T STOP HERE!

Discover more at www.capstonekids.com

- ♥ Videos & Contests
- ✿ Games & Puzzles
- ♥ Friends & Favorites
- ✿ Authors & Illustrators

Find cool websites and more books like this one at www.facthound.com. Just type in the Book ID: **9781404867567** and you're ready to go!